THIS AIN'T CHINATOWN

– A MURDER MYSTERY –

Fourth Book in the
Joe Zuma Murder Mystery Series

JEROME RABOW, PH.D.

ISBN 978-1-953223-05-0 (paperback)

Rushmore Press LLC
1 800 460 9188
www.rushmorepress.com

Printed in the United States of America

A DEDICATION

This fourth book in the *Joe Zuma Detective Series* is dedicated to all of the readers who have not yet met Zuma, his wife Claudia, or Zuma's sidekick Pat Vasquez. May these readers have as much pleasure discovering them as I have had creating them. I also wish to express my appreciation to the many readers who have told me about their enjoyment of plot and character.

Jerome Rabow

CHAPTER 1

Detective Joe Zuma smiled as the decayed corpses were being pulled into the shore by the Santa Monica Fire Department.

"What're you smiling at, boss? It's pretty ugly and gruesome looking to me. Those two bastards must have been in there for three or four days."

"I'm not smiling at what I see but what it makes me think of. This is right out of the film *Chinatown*! Did you see it, Pat? It's a great movie and there's a moment when Jack Nicholson watches a corpse being pulled out of the Los Angeles River. I remember so many scenes from that movie. The movie is about the struggle over water rights for LA. I don't think these corpses were involved in anything like that. Even though it's the ocean here and not the LA River, it looks like it could have been in the movie."

Zuma's assistant and right-hand man, Detective Pat Vasquez, admired his boss's memory of songs and movies and his ability to recall their narratives. In addition to being mentored about detective work, he was also learning about movies and music and often could repeat lyrics that Zuma sang. He admired and respected the ability that Zuma had to relate these everyday real-life situations of crime to artistic creations.

One corpse was wearing a blue denim jacket and had been shot in the head. The other corpse had two bullets, one that had entered the heart and the other the face. The detectives waited while both corpses were loaded into the waiting ambulance.

"I doubt if there is anything left in the clothing that will help us identify the guys. We'll have to wait till the coroner can get us some dental X-rays or DNA readings. I don't think we'll get fingerprints. Looks like the fish have been feasting. No, this is not about water rights, it's got to be about drugs, sex, adultery, or revenge."

It was Pat's turn to smile. He liked that his boss could make things sound simple although he and Zuma knew that this case was not going to be simple. Drugs, sex, adultery, or revenge never are.

As they were walking back, they heard a scream coming from a woman who was standing under the pier. She was pointing towards a body of a woman lying at the edge of the water, fully clothed, baldheaded, and wearing a necklace with a Star of David. The woman on shore was sobbing hysterically, but in between sobs, Zuma heard the name Maddie, and the lament of "how could this have happened to you, to us."

"Miss, I'm sorry to interrupt you. I'm Detective Zuma and this is my colleague Pat Vasquez. We're from the Santa Monica Police Department. You seem to know this person. If you could take a moment to calm down, we would like you to please tell us your name, her name, and what brought you down to the beach."

The woman continued to sob as she talked.

"I'm Abir Kouri. She is Marilyn Shankman. We live together. When Marilyn didn't come home last night, I began to worry and called your department. They said they had to wait seventy-two hours to file a missing person's report. I had trouble sleeping, and when her boss at the pharmacy where she works called and told me she hadn't come into work, I began to panic. I knew that the beach was her favorite spot, so I came down hoping to find here. Oh, God this is awful. Maddie, you are the love of my life. Maddie, Maddie, I pray to God this was not a rape."

"I gather that Marilyn was an orthodox Jew. She must have lost her wig in the ocean. If she was orthodox, she would not have been allowed to have a gay relationship. Can you help me understand your relationship? How long had you known each other?"

"When our families found out that we were gay they rejected us and told each of us to leave. We were lucky enough to meet at a meeting for religious people who were breaking away from their family because of strict orthodoxy. Even though I am Muslim, and she is or should I say was Jewish, we hit it off. We respected each other's religious beliefs and never let them interfere with our closeness. We had a lot in common: being professionals. I'm an assistant DA and Marilyn was a pharmacist. We liked people, loved our work, and been ambitious."

"I can understand where an ambitious DA might be heading but what is an ambitious pharmacist heading for?"

"She wanted to set up a chain of pharmacies that would sell drugs at a very low price. Her hope was to make medications more affordable for the poor. She knew the actual costs of drugs for the pharmaceutical companies, and she was outraged at the prices they charged."

"Do you know how far she had gotten with her plans for pharmacies or had she posted anything about the prices that might have upset the pharmaceutical companies?"

"She had developed a proposal for funding her plan. I think she wrote letters to the pharmaceutical companies. We were always writing letters. I wrote about discrepant incarceration rates, the unrepresentativeness of juries, and differences in arrest rates."

"Ms. Kouri, I know this must be a terrible shock to you, but you have been most helpful. We have to take her body to the morgue for identification and determine the exact cause of death. As soon as that is done, we will notify the family. Then we will call you. Please give us your telephone number so we can call and speak further, and could you also give us your phone so we may examine the calls you have made and received in the past three months."

"Here's my card and my phone, Detective. I want to be as helpful as possible. Feel free to call at any time."

"This isn't like another movie scene, is it, boss?"

"No, Pat, this scene is a reality scene about life in America for women and especially for orthodox women. They are hounded and ridiculed wherever they go, and men often feel justified in raping and killing them. Their dress seems to get some men very riled up. I think they get pissed off that the women are covering themselves up and defying how men want women to dress. They make for easy targets.

We're going to have to start with neighbors and find out what they can tell us about the two women—when they moved in and how they got along. Let's make sure to ask if they know of anyone who was upset that the women were in the building or in the neighborhood. Let's use their phones to see who they called. We'll call all the numbers for the last month. Pat, let's do the neighborhood and neighbors together."

"Boss, these three corpses, two males and one female, can't be connected. I know how you think, but this has gotta be a coincidence."

"Pat, you do know how I think and know I don't believe in coincidences, especially when it comes to murders that are close together in time or place."

When they got back to their precinct, Zuma called in three other officers.

"This is what we got. Three dead bodies: two males, one female. The female is identifiable. We'll wait on getting information on the males. In the interim, we need to start with the two women who were lovers and living together. We're going to give you pictures and their names. Williams, you go to the address and start with neighbors. Taylor, you go to the neighborhood and ask all shops in a one-mile radius about purchases and impressions. Hernandez, you check on all the phone numbers called and the incoming ones on their phones. You can't indicate that there has been a murder. We have to notify next of kin first. You indicate that an investigation is being conducted and you are gathering as much information as possible. We're going to give you their pictures and names. Any questions? Good, let's get started."

"Boss, you left out their places of work."

"You and I are going to do that, Pat. These were two very accomplished women. One was a district attorney and the other was a pharmacist. Can you imagine how much they had to struggle to get to that place? Tough enough to be a woman in that male world but to also be orthodox meant they must have been smart, disciplined, and focused. And I guarantee that one still is. We need to find out everything we can about their work and relationships at work."

"What a way to start a Monday, boss."

Zuma took out one of the toothpicks that he always kept in his left shirt pocket and started humming.

"Yeah, Pat, that's what the Mamas and the Papas said."

"What do you mean, boss? Who are the Mamas and the Papas? What song were you humming?"

"They were one of the best singing groups of the sixties. The words I'm thinking of refer to not being able to trust Monday morning. The song is simply called, 'Monday, Monday.' When they sing 'Monday, Monday, So Good to Me,' it's sarcastic because the singer can't guarantee that the lover will be there on Monday evening. People are coming back, fresh from a weekend, looking forward to a new week, and you just can't trust Monday morning to put you in or keep your good mood. Pat, there are lots of versions since it was such a huge hit, but the Mamas and Papas version is my favorite."

"I see what the connection is, boss. It's Monday morning and we can't guarantee anything for these corpses except a funeral."

Pat was not upset about it being Monday morning and having three corpses to deal with. He was worried about a problem unrelated to the crime that related to his neighbor. He began clicking his tongue against his gums.

"Is something bothering you, Pat? What's the matter?"

"Oh, nothing important, boss."

Pat did not feel he wanted to talk about the problem he was having feeling it was minor compared to the feelings he had about being uplifted on learning about a great movie and a song that he was looking forward to listening to. It was always a plus for Pat to get introduced to songs and music he knew nothing about. Once again, he admired his boss for connecting the real-life situations of crime and murder that they faced every day to an artistic creation.

Zuma decided not to press Pat for details knowing that the tongue clicking meant he was absorbed in something unrelated to the crime but also knowing that in time Pat would probably talk to him about what was on his mind.

CHAPTER 2

The pharmacy Marilyn Shankman had worked at was on Lincoln Avenue and Rose in a split mall. It was not an upscale area of Santa Monica. Zuma and Pat walked in, went up to the manager's window, saw the nameplate of Slavkin, identified themselves, and asked about Marilyn Shankman.

"Marilyn is a very reliable employee and always upbeat. People who work here called her 'Merrilyn.' It is quite unusual that I hadn't heard from her this morning. She always called if she was ill or running late, which she rarely was. No, she didn't seem to have any strange habits. I know she had to leave early on Friday nights to go to her temple, and she would not work on Saturdays but those were the only things about her other than her cheeriness that I noticed. She was my best employee. When she didn't come in this morning, I called her cell phone but got no answer, so I left a message. Should I be worried? Can you tell me what this is about? Am I going to have to find a replacement for her? You can't find people like her anymore."

"Mr. Slavkin. If you don't mind, we'd like to speak with a few of your other employees."

"No, not at all. Here are the numbers of others who are not at the counter now but who have worked with her. Please tell me what this is about."

"Right now, all we can tell you is that it is just an investigation. And can you check her files to see whom she listed as persons to get in touch with if anything were to happen to her. Please email the information to me and once we know something more definite, we will get back to you."

The phone calls made to the two other pharmacists who were not on duty reported the same information about Marilyn Shankman. She was always cheerful, very cooperative, concerned with their personal problems and willing to pinch-hit if they couldn't come in because of a childcare or other personal issue.

"Gee, boss, no one with grudges at work. She sounds like a great person."

"She sure does, Pat. Let's head back to the station. The courthouse is close by, and we can visit the DA."

Chief DA John Delany was surprised to hear there was an investigation related to Abir Kouri.

"I never have to worry if she is not here when we open shop in the morning. I know she is on the job and probably interviewing witnesses. Right now, she's on a case where she is finding it difficult for witnesses to come forward. She is defending a fifteen-year-old kid who was caught selling meth, but her feeling is the kid was pressured to do this by some dealer. The witnesses she was trying to get were from the neighborhood. She wanted parents or kids to testify that the dealer was a frequent visitor to the neighborhood. No one was cooperating. She knew everyone must be in fear of their lives, but I knew she would be relentless. She is one of my best attorneys. I always know she's going to be careful on a case but also diligent."

"Can you check her file to see who you might have to notify if something would happen to her?"

"Sure, no problem, Detective. I can get that for you in a second. I'll pull up her personnel file. Let's see, she wants Mordechai and Bella Kouri. They must be her parents. And there is one other name, Marilyn Shankman."

"Pat, let's visit the Shankmans first, then the Kouris. We should let Slavkin know he'll have to find a replacement. We need to deliver the bad news, and the sooner we do that the better it will be for our guys to say they are conducting a murder investigation. They might get better information. After that, we can call it a day. On a happier note, would you like to have dinner with Claudia and me?"

Pat nodded yes. He was always delighted to dine with the two of them. They were very much in love after five years, and he admired the way they spoke and listened to each other.

"Hi, honey, I'd like Pat to join us for dinner tonight. We got some new cases today. If you want to go somewhere besides the Shangri-La, make a reservation. Seven should work."

"Pat, I'll take the Kouris and you do the interview with the Shankmans. Your experience dating the last woman made you a bit of an expert on Judaism so that should help us.

CHAPTER 3

Mrs. Shankman looked through the peephole and when she saw two men, she went to get her husband, knowing she was not allowed to be alone in a room with men. When the Shankmans ushered them in, Mr. Shankman invited the two detectives to be seated.

"Mr. and Mrs. Shankman, do you have any idea why we might be here?"

Before Mrs. Shankman could open her mouth, Mr. Shankman replied, "I assume it's about our daughter or rather it's about a person who used to be our daughter. We disowned her when she disobeyed our most sacrilegious of tenets. We no longer consider her to be our daughter."

"I'm sorry to inform you that the woman you no longer consider to be your daughter was found dead this morning in the water off the Santa Monica Beach."

Mrs. Shankman screamed as Mr. Shankman dropped his jaw but also tried to muzzle his wife. He spoke without affect.

"Our God has punished her. We warned her not to disobey."

"Mr. and Mrs. Shankman, the death of a child is the worst nightmare a parent can have. Detective Vasquez and I are sorry for your terrible loss."

"You might be interested to know that she was a very successful pharmacist, well-liked by her coworkers and boss."

"That's not important to us. I'm sure it is also not important to God."

"I know this must be a shock at a time like this, but we would like to ask you a few questions. Your answers might help us gain some understanding of this crime. Can you tell us the date when you disowned your daughter, Mr. Shankman?"

"It is not a problem for us to talk. For us she has been dead since before we disowned her. She was dead when she told us about her violation of our sacred commandment about lying with a member of the same sex. We disowned her about a year ago when she told us she would be living with her girlfriend. I think it was about November 2018."

"What was her life like growing up with the two of you?"

"She was always challenging me and the rules I had about living the life our God commands. She didn't like the way I treated my wife and was always urging her mother to challenge me. She always questioned the Commandments and often said they were stupid and outdated. She created fights and arguments between my wife and me."

"That must have been very difficult for you, Mr. Shankman. I understand that you've had no contact with her or her friends, but if you can think of anyone who might have wanted to hurt your daughter, please let us know."

"Did she have any enemies?"

"I assume God would have created lots of enemies for her since she defied his sacraments."

"Stop it, Herschel. Our daughter was sweet and kind. No one ever disliked her."

"Was there someone in your community who was angry or upset with Marilyn's choices?"

"We didn't talk about her behavior. If someone knew they never discussed it with me. Did anyone talk to you, Mimi?"

"No, Herschel. I would have told you if anyone did."

"Mr. and Mrs. Shankman, thank you for your cooperation. If we learn new things about her death how would you prefer for to be contacted?"

"Don't bother, Detective. For us, she has been dead for a year."

"For you, Herschel, she has been dead, but not for me. I want to see her body. I can give her a proper burial."

"Mimi, you are forbidden to do that. They will not allow her in our cemetery. I am forbidding you to do anything. She has been dead for a long time."

"*I will not obey you. I'm tired of obeying you.* I can and will do somethings that satisfies me, and that I must do. I can make sure she is wrapped in a proper shroud. I can bring in men, even if I have to go to prison to get them for the mourning period. You have been forbidding me for over forty years. No more. Not about our daughter. If it is not in our cemetery, it will be one that I can go to and visit."

"Thank you both. I will call you or you can call me to find out when the coroner has finished. Here is my card."

"Boss, that husband is one of the coldest Jews I've ever known. When I was with my Jewish girlfriend, I learned how Jews like to have their loved ones buried. I went to several different funerals, and I was really impressed how they went about celebrating the life of the person who had died rather than mourning the death. They acknowledged faults and violations but were never punitive. I was shocked to hear how upset he was about the violation of their basic tenets. Boy, he is one tough cookie."

"Orthodoxy makes you rigid, Pat. It allows you to act on principle and not on or about a person. I was that way at one time and thank God Claudia helped me change."

"I never knew you were religious, boss."

"I wasn't, Pat. I was rigid about discovering the guilty and what they deserved. I'll explain it to you over dinner. Let's get to the Kouris."

The Kouris were more welcoming than the Shankmans.

"We believed that when our daughter told us she was gay that it would be a temporary thing. We said she would always be welcome in our home, but we would not be telling our friends. We did not want her living under the same roof believing that she would continue to sin. We simply told everyone that her work as a district attorney was keeping her very busy."

"So, in this past year, had you ever seen or spoken to her?"

"I went to court once and sat in the back. I was very proud of how she could stand up to those bad men. I left before the trial ended so we did not speak. Mordechai, I am sorry that I did not tell you."

"Would you have any knowledge of anyone who would want to harm your daughter?"

"I think any of those bad men that she put away would be wanting to seek revenge. Is she in some kind of trouble?"

"No, not that we know of. We would like to call on you again if we have new questions. Thank you for your help today."

"Pat this has been a full day. Three bodies, one of which is female, two families and no suspects. Let's go to dinner. Talking to Claudia might help.

"Hi, Claudia. Sure, go ahead and finish up the painting you're working on. Thank you for making the reservations. Pat and I will wait for you at the restaurant and have a drink. Take an Uber so we can drive home together. See you at seven."

As Zuma and Pat sat in the Shangri-La bar waiting for Claudia, Pat decided this would be a good time to talk to his boss.

"What I was thinking about the other day is this problem I'm having with my neighbor. He plays his music really loud, keeps me up when I'm going to bed, and sometimes he plays it very early in the morning, like 2:00 a.m., so it wakes me. It's never the kind of music that you sing or teach me about. It doesn't seem to have a melody, and I just get a steady pounding beat. I have asked him to tone it down and he refuses, telling me it's a free country. I have been hesitant to tell him I'm a detective since he might think I'm harassing him and he would report me. I'm also hesitant to call our precinct since the guys who would show up would think I'm a wimp and I would become the laughingstock of the precinct. I don't know what to do!"

Zuma laughed and took a slow sip of his vodka martini.

"Those neighborly problems can be the most difficult to handle. I hated when I got those kinds of calls before I got promoted to detective and happy that I don't have to deal with them anymore. They have the potential for being extended well beyond the original complaint. If the guy stops because of your complaint and is angry, he may start to do other things that will upset you, but you won't know he's doing it. Oh, look who's walking in. Pat, let me think about it some more. I'll get back to you in a day or so."

Pat felt good about talking to Zuma about his predicament and greeted Claudia warmly and with a kiss on her cheek.

CHAPTER 4

"Tell me, boss, about your rigidity when it came to criminals."

"Pat, I was pretty sure that I had a suspect whom I knew had killed her husband. I was planning to turn all the evidence over to the DA, and I was pretty sure she was going to be convicted. There was a problem though. The woman had a daughter that Claudia had been working with at school. You also knew her. When I told Claudia that I was going to go to the district attorney and that there would probably be a prison sentence, Claudia said it would ruin the child's life and began arguing and pleading with me not to do it. Claudia and I locked horns. I can still hear her words.

'You can't go after her. If you get solid evidence and she is convicted what will happen to Lucy? There is no one else in the family. She will be handed over to foster care. And she's now a kid whose mother is a murderer. Other kids will chew her up and make mincemeat of her. She will be hounded and humiliated. That's too much for any child to handle. She has lost a father, a teacher and now could lose her mother. Joe, you need to have mercy on this kid.'

"Pat, you could understand my conflict. You know that we have to take an oath to pursue the guilty. That is our job. That is what we do. I could not let murderers walk around scot-free.

'You need to put mercy on those scales of justice, Joe. This is not like you. This is not your best self. She's already lived two years scot-free. What is wrong with more years? Not every crime is solved.'

"I had never been confronted with anything like this in all the years I had been a detective. Someone was asking me to not pursue someone who I was 99 percent sure was goddamn guilty. If this were a higher up, even a mayor, I would refuse to accept that directive. But this was Claudia, the woman I loved. Then she laid it out as to what she would do.

'Joe, if you go forward, I will seek to adopt her. If she comes into our life, she will never accept you. She will come between us. Please don't do this. She is an innocent. Not an innocent adult who can eventually understand but an innocent child.'

"I felt she was making me choose between the woman I loved and my integrity. She convinced me when she said to me that 'in her eyes, I would have more integrity if I give up my pursuit. Pat, she made me see my integrity would now include mercy. But she really clinched it for me when she showed me what might have happened to me if I had acted in a similar manner."

'Joe, remember when you told me how angry you were that your wife got killed. Suppose you had done something in revenge, and you were sent away. What do you think that would have done to your children, knowing that their father murdered someone?'

"I can only imagine. It would have been horrendous. It probably would have wrecked their lives."

'Yes, and you would have been haunted by the idea of what you had done to your children. I believe that this woman whom you want to put away must sometimes feel the same way.'

"Maybe you're right."

'The woman did something out of revenge. What you're doing now is preventing a life from being wrecked.'

"So that's my story Pat. I am the better person and the better detective because of her. My rigidity was broken by her helping me empathize with another parent who did something out of revenge as I might have done."

"That's quite a story, boss. Is the woman around today?"

"Yes, she is, Pat, and from what I have heard, she is doing all kinds of wonderful things. She volunteers in a woman's shelter and teaches woodwork to women who want to develop a craft and become furniture makers. I don't feel bad or guilty about the decision I made. Good and wonderful things happened because of Claudia's wisdom.

And here comes my wonderful woman. Hi, darling, I was just telling Pat how you made me into a better person and a better detective."

"It was easy, Joe. You were already very good at both."

Zuma and Pat spent the rest of the evening providing details of the murders of the two women and the one man to Claudia, who became increasingly pensive as they spoke.

"I don't have any thoughts about the men. The details about the women disturbs me. I've seen and read a lot about women who try and get away from cults and orthodox communities. There was a program on TV about Scientology and another one about the Chassidics in Brooklyn and what they did to young men who they discovered were gay. Those communities seem to be capable of doing anything to their own when they are threatened or afraid of the behavior or departure of one of their own. Maybe that is what is involved here. It is a commentary on our species that animals rarely abandon their young while humans can and do."

"Do you see the advantages, Pat, of being married to a smart woman?"

"I do, boss, and if she's right, we have a lot more potential suspects than just the families."

"Claudia, do you think the two women being very accomplished, one a pharmacist and the other an assistant district attorney, had had anything to do with the crime?"

"Accomplished women, if they leave, threaten orthodox communities. If they stay its fine."

"OK, my accomplished partner. You have never threatened me. However, you have made a lot more work for Pat and me, and we're going to have to start early tomorrow morning. We must leave. Good night, Pat. I've got the tab."

CHAPTER 5

It didn't take long for Pat to trace the missing person's report that had been filed by a person whose first name was Carmela.

"Boss, we finally tracked down the tattooed body's connection. Her missing person's report said that her father had a tattoo with her name on his chest. She works in a woman's dress boutique and was eager to meet with us as soon as possible after she finished work at seven. I asked her if she gets off at her lunch hour and she suggested a new piazza place that just opened and was offering a discount. Address is 1521 Vine in Hollywood. It's called 800 Piazza. She didn't want to travel west. Something about her car. Her last name is Lopez."

"Ms. Lopez, we're sorry to inform you that your father was found in the Pacific Ocean off the Santa Monica Pier. He had been shot. We are lucky he had the tattoo with your name. We were able to find you after you filed the missing person's report with the same name. What can you tell us about your dad and your relationship with him?"

"I always expected he would end up like you found him. My dad was a very good father. He and my mother split because she was an alcoholic. I was sixteen and moved in with him. He paid for everything. When I stopped going to college and told him my dream, he didn't lecture me on my quitting school but supported what I wanted which was to own my own dress shop. From since I was twelve, he had been putting $50 a week into a savings account.

I'm now thirty-two. For twenty years, he has been the most reliable dad in the world. I now have about $50,000 in savings, but I need $100,000 to get started."

"How often would you see him? Did he tell you how he made a living?"

"No, I didn't see him much after I left home. We met twice a month for dinner, and he would give me some extra cash. He never told me how he earned money. I'm smart enough to know it had to be something fishy. He told me I would be better off not knowing."

"Ms. Lopez, do you have any idea of why your dad was murdered? Or who could have done it?"

"Fishy businesses, Detective, have fishy endings. As I said a moment ago, my father said I was better off not knowing, and I have no idea of whom he knew, worked with, or what he did. I wish I could help you more than I have. Thank you for coming down. Would it be okay if I asked some questions?"

"Sure, Ms. Lopez, fire away."

"My questions are for Detective Vasquez. Detective Vasquez, do you speak Spanish?"

"I'm afraid I don't. My parents insisted I learn English, and I was not allowed to use Spanish at home."

"That's too bad. My Dad was proud of his heritage. Insisted I had to learn about it or else I would end up whitewashed. When we went out, it was always to really good Mexican restaurants, El Coyote, Le Talpa. We saw movies made in Mexico. And he even took me to theatres that were doing Mexican productions.

"Detective Vasquez do you know about the Zoot suits? Just in case you don't know, service men and white civilians attacked and stripped children, teenagers, and youths who wore Zoot suits. Why? Because they considered the outfits, made from a lot of fabric, unpatriotic during World War II since rationing of fabric was required at the time. Those attacks were rooted in racism against Mexicans and Mexican Americans. Detective Vasquez, do you think that you are whitewashed?"

Vasquez and Zuma laughed and admired her brashness.

"I don't think so."

"Would you like to learn Spanish? I could teach you. No charge. We can start lessons after I get off at work at seven. I'll also throw in some other history lessons like the Sleepy Lagoon murder in 1942 and the high school students at Garfield High School who started the Chicano power movement and the brown berets. Do you still believe you are not whitewashed?"

"You may have a point Ms. Lopez."

"I know I have a point and I could make several more. When do you want to start lessons?"

"I couldn't do anything with you until this case is solved."

"Well, here's hoping to a quick solution. Here's my home phone, Detective Vasquez. I look forward to your call. Thank you both for coming across town."

"Could you give us an address for your father?"

"Here's the last address I had for my father. He moved around a lot."

"Pat, she is definitely AIO."

"What's that boss?'

"**After**, **In** and **On** to you. Pat, would you like me to tell you about that Sleepy Lagoon murder? It was a very shameful event in Los Angeles policing."

"Boss, I think I have had enough history lessons for today. But I was wondering if you had a chance to think a bit more about current events, like the problem with my neighbor."

"I have, Pat. I spoke to Claudia about it because I know you know that she would not think you're a wimp. She and I came up with the 'kill them with kindness' idea. The idea is that you disarm his defensiveness by offering to do something very kind or, in your case, we just call it neighborly. You can offer to take out his garbage once a week or tell him you'd be willing to pick up the mail or do some shopping for him. I'm not sure how many things you can do for a neighbor in an apartment building, but I think you get the idea."

"I do, boss, and I will think about it. Thank you, and please thank Claudia when you see her."

CHAPTER 6

The coroners' report was on Zuma's desk when he arrived. Death had occurred prior to the drowning. He had been shot with a .38 caliber Glock and there were powder burns on the body. Two fingerprints were traceable, and they do have some X-rays of dental work. If the guy had a record, they should have an ID by this afternoon.

"Pat, when someone is shot this close, it means the vic and the killer or killers could have been a friend or someone in the same business. Let's run the files for corpses who have been shot with that caliber weapon in the past four years."

"Boss, Williams, Taylor, and Hernandez are waiting in the other room."

"All the neighbors raved about them and were very upset about what happened. They spoke how friendly and helpful they were. Always willing to babysit if an emergency came up and in a couple of cases, they tutored some of the neighbor's kids."

"Taylor, I have a feeling the shops will report something very similar."

"You're right, sir. All the shop owners and the clerks reported how polite and friendly they were. They knew the names of all the clerks and in some cases brought presents for the clerks' children."

"Hernandez, you can't be less helpful than your buddies. What did you find checking on the phone numbers?"

"We found that the Jewish gal had a weekly conversation with her mother. There was one other number that was dialed often. It was to a person with the same last name, Nathan Shankman. Could be her brother. We're getting his address now as we speak. He has a record for drug dealing."

"Good work, all of you. I think we need to go back to the Shankmans and find out why they did not talk about their son. Let's be careful, those calls between the mother and her children may have been made without the father's knowledge."

———m———

"Mrs. Shankman, we would like to speak with you again."

"I will let you in, but you can't tell my husband. He would be furious if he knew I was in a room alone with men."

"Mrs. Shankman, I know this is not a good time for you to talk but can you tell us about why you didn't mention your son when we last spoke?"

"It would have infuriated my husband more than it did when you brought up our daughter. Nathan was a bigger disappointment to my husband than our daughter. He was, not only disobedient, but he was stealing from us and using the money for drugs. He would not speak with our rabbi and finally we disowned him."

"But we have a record of your phone calls to both of your children."

"I know. I found it too difficult to not have contact with them and felt horrible and guilty about disowning both our children."

"When you spoke with Nathan last what did he tell you?"

"He said that he was into a business deal that would be very lucrative and that he would be sending us money. I knew it couldn't be kosher and told him we didn't need or want his money. I was worried because he had never shared anything before about what he was doing. He was excited, so I knew that it might mean trouble."

"Did he say what kind of business deal it might be?"

"Nathan's businesses have always been about stealing and drugs. It had to be trouble. I was scared. But I couldn't tell my husband. I called my daughter. She said she would speak with him."

"And what were your weekly conversations with your daughter about?"

"They were mother-daughter talks. She talked about her work and how pleased she was to be involved putting bad people away, and of course, she talked about her relationship with Abir and how well they were doing. She wanted me to meet with them, but I was afraid my husband would find out. I regret that I let my fear of him prevent me from seeing them."

—m—

"Pat, the worst thing in the world is to lose a child. Guaranteed to break your heart."

"Boss, we're at ground zero with this Shankman murder. The only connections are the girlfriend, the brother, and the parents. I don't think anyone at work was upset with her or had anything to gain. And I don't believe the father could have or would have done it. As far as he was concerned both of his children were dead. That leaves the brother and the girlfriend. But I don't see any motives there."

"You're right, Pat. We have to get back to the lawyer. Perhaps the cases she was working on had something to do with the murder, and she may know something about Marilyn's brother. Pat, please call ahead to see if she can see us."

As Pat was dialing the number, he heard Zuma humming a song that he didn't recognize.

"Is that a new one, boss? I don't recognize it."

"No, Pat, it's quite an oldie. It's called "How Can You Mend A Broken Heart," The words suggest that a broken heart would be harder to mend than stopping the rain from falling down or the sun from shining."

"I've never known that kind of pain, boss."

"Hopefully, Pat, you never will."

CHAPTER 7

When Zuma arrived home that night, he found Claudia quite distraught.

"I got in trouble at school today. I ended up screaming at four boys."

"What happened?"

"These upper classmen, they must have been twelve or thirteen, were bullying two younger girls. They were in second grade, and I had worked with these two very sweet and quite talented kids. One girl who was slightly overweight was being called all kinds of names and the other girl for the clothing she was wearing. The boys were relentless. The girls didn't know what to say. They didn't know how to respond and began crying, which egged the bullies on to the point that they began making remarks about the families of the girls and how their parents must be ashamed. I lost it, Joe. Here was innocence being destroyed right in front of me. Here was the beginning of girls coming to understand that it is a man's world. Here was a scene, right in my workplace, which I knew would be enacted in classrooms, schoolyards, dormitories, and workplaces all over America and even all over the world. I separated the boys from the girls and lined them up against a wall. I asked them what their parents would do or say if they knew what they had done. They were silent and hung their heads down. I asked them to pick up their heads, look at me, and tell me what it was that bothered them.

"We don't like fat girls. We don't like girls who dress like boys."

"Well, I don't like bullies and people who take advantage of smaller and younger people. So, since you're such big shots, why don't you call me names."

They were silent.

"Are you afraid."

You're not fat and you dress nicely."

"That's not why you're silent like a lamb. No, you're afraid of someone who has authority."

"I began screaming into their faces.

'You are little pick squeaks who go after youngers.'

"At this point some other teacher pulled me away. I had to go to the principal's office, and he reprimanded me for losing control. I agreed, but I told him he had to do something about the bullying that goes on in our school. He thought for a while and agreed.

'And I'd like you to be in charge of the training for teachers and for the children.'"

"So, it ended up pretty good."

"It did, Joe. But I am ashamed of how I bullied those boys. All I could see was that these privileged brats would be doing this same crap later on with their girlfriends and secretaries and wives. These were not brown or black or girls who were recent immigrants to our country. They were also privileged, but it did not matter to these boys. They were girls and that was sufficient for them to use their power and privilege to target and abuse."

"We all lose it some days, Claudia. You'll make up for it. I know you are going to turn those boys around as you have often turned me around."

"Thanks, Joe. The principal must have been waiting for someone else to start this. He probably felt he could not initiate it on his own. He is giving me extra money to conduct the training first for teachers and then for the students. He is also going to have a retreat for the kids and parents are going to be strongly urged to participate. I guess I have an ally, Joe."

"More than one Claudia, more than one."

CHAPTER 8

Zuma and Pat had no trouble getting in to see Abir Kouri. Their call had paved the way and they stood waiting for her to motion them in. As they peered through the glass, they saw the stack of folders in the in box and the twenty or more cardboard boxes on the floor with case numbers on them. They commented to each other on the heavy caseload and the kind of commitment she must have.

"Thanks for taking a moment to see us, Ms. Kouri. It looks like you have a heavy caseload. We wanted to let you know that we have nothing on anyone as yet, but we identified the other body. He has a record of drug dealing. He used a number of aliases in his dealings with the law. Here is his picture. Does he look familiar to you? We were wondering if you had any knowledge of him or actual dealings with him in your practice."

"Hmm. I think so"

She went over to a shelf and pulled down a folder.

"Yes, he was picked up for drug dealing. Nathan Shankman was with this known drug dealer. We figured the other guy was the connection and making sure Nathan, he used the name Norman, was going to be okay in the neighborhood. The guy was black. Norman or Nathan was white. The guy was saying to the kids, 'You can buy from this guy. He's my man and not a dick.' One of your detectives spotted the two of them and picked them up. The guy was clean and said he was just walking by and watching what was going on. Norman or Nathan was fined and put on probation. The guy who we know has a big record for dealing was also fined for violating his probation and being in the presence of a drug dealer. His name was Calvin Grand. They both had good legal representation."

"Your boss told us you're involved in trying to get witnesses to come forward and testify for you. Could you tell us a little more about this case?"

"Sure. I'm guessing you both know that the inner city is where drugs are pushed. I know that the Westside and Santa Monica are high in drug use, but it's more often recreational than for addiction. That doesn't make it any better, but those folks are not likely to break more laws or steal to support their usage. The kids are prey to pushers. They become addicted and need money to support their habit. The pushers are glad to help if the kids work for them. There are few playgrounds, afterschool programs, and the community members are scared to point out the pushers. Nathan must have known he would be safe from being reported. This kid who I was called in to prosecute was bright, had good grades, and I felt I could get through to him and get him to talk if I offered him a good deal. His name is Thomas, Thomas Barnes. I told him I could get him transferred to a new school, get him tutoring, and a job for his mom. He is wavering. If I get him to talk it could mean that we would be putting one big dealer out of business."

"This is a wild speculation, Ms. Kouri, but do you see any possibility that this Thomas kid and Nathan are connected?"

"Not so wild, Detective. The young man was under the thumb of the same man who was introducing Nathan to the community. He is the man who you found strangled on the beach."

"So, if this dealer was murdered, do you think the kid is also in danger?"

"I didn't until a moment ago when you identified the vic. Can you get some witness protection for the kid right now? He might still be in school. Here's his home address."

"Pat, take the car, get to the school, and put the lights and sirens on. This could be crucial. I'll take an Uber back to the precinct. Thank you, Ms. Kouri. You've been most helpful and I'm sure we will be seeing each other more."

On the drive back, Zuma had his toothpick out and was wondering what advantage is there to having a dealer killed? Who would benefit from that? It couldn't be anyone from his family. Would it be someone from the community? Would it be another competitive drug dealer? As he was walking into the precinct, a call came from Pat.

"We're too late, boss. The kid was shot inside the schoolyard while he was playing basketball. It had to be a good shooter. Three bullets to the chest. No one else is hurt. No one is talking. The school is in lockdown."

"Shit, Pat, we're in the same goddamn business as heart surgeons. Seconds count and we lost this one. I'm coming down with some others. We're going to bring in the trauma crew."

<hr>

In the auditorium, after a member of the team had stressed how important it was to talk about feelings, no one spoke. Zuma, knowing in advance that he would get no response, asked if anyone saw the car and if anyone did would they come in and talk to him. He said that no one would ever find out who identified the car. There was silence. The principal spoke.

"You can all go home early or if you want to stay in the auditorium and study that would be fine."

After most of the kids left, the principal, Mr. Carl Edwards, asked Zuma and Pat to come into his office.

"I'm getting used to these. In the past year, we have had four shootings on my school grounds. Nothing we do seems to stop it. Guards, metal detectors, locked gates. It's a goddamn hopeless cause. The kids are frightened. The parents are frightened. We are in a prison. And the dealers are running it."

"Mr. Edwards, I'll get some of my minority officers to go into the neighborhood. We can try again to get a parent to talk. Someone may realize that their kid might be next unless something is done."

"Thanks, Detective. I'm going to have to visit the parents of Thomas. I'm sure he had some things in his locker."

"Mr. Edwards, we need to take the vic down to the morgue. We will have to bring in the parents for a positive identification. You can probably get to visit them tomorrow. Even though we know who the young man was, we will need a positive identification from the parents."

"Boss, that poor guy sees a lot of dead kids. That's got to be an awfully tough job."

"It is, Pat. All inner-city principals have it tough and it looks like it will continue that way for a long time. Pat, I've got a better idea than the one I told him about. Let's get the Barnes kid down to the morgue and then head back to the precinct. Will you call Abir Kouri? Tell her to meet us and that we have an idea on how we can help her."

"Here's what we can do, Ms. Kouri. We can put one of our younger-looking black officers into the school. I can get papers that will identify him as a transfer student. He might be able to sniff out who is getting kids to sell drugs. We can also send an officer to talk to the parents of the young man who was killed. They might have nothing to lose at this point."

"I like all of those ideas. Can you also send a few officers to ask other parents if they would be willing to testify? Will you let the principal know who the undercover agent is?"

"Good idea. I can find some others to knock on doors. You're the only one outside of the department who will know we have an undercover person in the school. Pat, let Ms. Kouri meet our guy now. She should know who he is in case something comes up in the school."

CHAPTER 9

Zuma and Pat found Mrs. Thomas at home, and when she opened the door, they could see she had been sobbing.

"Mrs. Thomas, thank you so much for meeting with us. I know this is a terrible time for you, but if you can answer some questions now, we may be able to find out who killed your son."

"Oh, I know who killed him. I was afraid to go to the police before because I knew I'd be in danger. Now, I have nothing to lose. My Thomas had been hounded by a big black man. I told Thomas to keep away from him, but I guess the guy kept after him and would meet him after school hours. After he stopped coming, this white guy would come around, and he and Thomas would go outside. I figured he was giving Thomas drugs to sell, but Thomas said he knew what he was doing and wouldn't listen to me saying to stop."

"Here is a picture, Mrs. Thomas. Could you identify this man as the one who was coming around to your home to speak with Thomas?"

"Yes, Detective. That white man is the one. I'm very sure he's the one who kept coming around after the black man stopped."

Zuma had no trouble finding Nathan Shankman. When they picked him up and told him he was wanted for the investigation of the murder, he became silent. At the precinct, Zuma had set it up so that Mrs. Shankman and her son would be seated across from one another.

"You, Mr. Shankman, have lost a sister and you, Mrs. Shankman, have lost a son. We would like to find the killer or killers of Marilyn and could use any help you can provide."

"I have no ideas, Detective."

"Nathan, I beg you to be honest with the detective."

"Mom, I don't know anything."

"Nathan, that is not exactly true. We have pictures of you selling drugs with the man who was murdered, so you knew the man. When was the last time you spoke to Mr. Grand?"

"I don't remember."

"Nathan, here's the deal. I can subpoena your phone and check all the numbers you called and received. If one of the numbers comes up that turns out to be the one that belongs to Mr. Grand, I'm going to charge you with "withholding information" and "being an accessory to a murder" and possibly two, including your sister."

"My son would have never done that to his sister. He is not a great kid, but he is not a murderer."

"My mom is right, Detective. Murder has never been my thing."

"So, if you're not, who do you think murdered Grand? And who murdered your sister?"

"For Grand, it could have been a competitor. I have no idea about who would have wanted to kill my sister."

"Nathan, tell us how you were involved with Mr. Grand. And tell us who found out that you had a sister who worked in a pharmacy. Who might have known or figured that out?"

"You probably have a good idea already. When you picked me up with him, I was selling drugs that he had obtained for me. He was introducing me to the neighborhood so that they would not be suspicious of me, the white dude who was really an undercover spy looking for kids selling drugs. We had a nice deal going. I accidentally told him that my sister was a pharmacist, and he asked me if she would be open to getting him drugs either cheaply or illegally. I told him absolutely not. She was a very honest person. He asked me where she worked. I lied and said I wasn't sure. He must have tracked her down. It probably wasn't that hard to find where a Shankman was working in a pharmacy. That was the last conversation I had with him. My sister called me when she got a visit from a man who said he knew me, and she asked if I knew him. I asked her to describe the guy and when she did, I told her yes, I did know him and that she had to be very, very careful. She asked if I was in danger and I told her no."

"When did she call you?"

"The day before she was murdered."

"So, your motive in murdering Mr. Grand would be to protect your sister. Your noose is getting tighter, Mr. Shankman. There's a body and a motive. Now we just need to find the weapon. Even without a weapon, there's enough evidence that a jury might indict you"

"I know it looks bad for me, but I did not kill Grand. He was my supplier."

"Your mom said that you were into a big deal and going do make a lot of money. Can you tell us what that was about?"

"Grand said he had lined up more kids from another two schools, and that he was going to introduce me. I would be able to triple my earnings."

"Nathan, I told you we didn't need the money. You are hurting innocent children, children who have so many other things going against them. They don't need you to add drugs to their lives. Please stop. I beg you."

"Mom, someone else will take my place."

"At least I would know it's not you."

"Unfortunately, Mrs. Shankman, your son is right. The inner city is the area where the pushers go and look for kids that they can seduce with money. Nathan, I'm not going to book you now. We're going to put an ankle bracelet on so we can monitor your whereabouts. We're still investigating Grand's murder. A young man in the school where you were pushing drugs was murdered. His name is Thomas Barnes. Did you kill him?"

"Absolutely not, detectives. I liked that kid, and I would do nothing to hurt him."

"Yeah, except get him involved in selling drugs."

After letting Nathan and his mother leave, Zuma and Pat headed back to the precinct.

"Boss, I don't think he killed the kid but I'm not sure about Grand."

"I agree, Pat. We need to see if we can find anything from our agent in the school."

Pat heard Zuma humming after the toothpick came out.

"That's another one that I don't know."

"It's a weird song to be humming at this time, Pat. It's a song that celebrates how often love and sex occur, and for some reason, I'm thinking of how often these schools prove to be fertile grounds for drug pushers."

"What are the words boss?"

"I'm embarrassed to say, Pat, but some cute lines are

> *Birds do it, bees do it. Even educated fleas do it.*
> *Some Argentines, without means do it.*
> *People say in Boston even beans do it.*
> *Let's do it, let's fall in love."*

"Those are cute lines, boss. I guess you and I know that drug pushers will keep doing it."

"They sure will, Pat. It's a cute song that for some weird, unexplainable reason I'm humming to describe a terrible situation,"

"Yeah, boss, cute songs and terrible situations don't belong together."

CHAPTER 10

The detectives had been knocking on the doors, asking witnesses to look at the photographs they provided and indicate if they had seen Nathan Shankman or Carl Grand. They found four parents who were willing to say they knew them from seeing them and that they would be willing to testify. Their sentiments had grown to the point where they were fed up and understood that if no one stepped up, the killings would continue. All of them had sons. The undercover agent in the school found three students who were selling, but they had not spilled who their dealer was. He gave the names and addresses to Zuma who asked that they be followed. A week of tracking the kids did not uncover any contacts with outsiders but did reveal that the kids were still selling. Zuma and Pat felt their best bet would be to pick up the three, show them the footage they had on their selling to fellow students, threaten them with juvenile hall or worse, and ask them to identify their dealer or else…. The kids were separated and told that their fellow sellers had given a name and was going to get off and unless they did the same; they were in trouble. One of the three identified the dealer. When Zuma and Pat asked the others to verify the person they did. It was Mr. Edwards.

"You got me, Detective. I knew that dealers would want everyone in my school to become addicted. I felt by controlling the number of drugs I gave to the kids it would limit the addictions. I thought I was doing something that would have some positive impact. Fewer kids in my school would get hooked."

"Mr. Edwards, in all my years of dealing with crime and criminal behavior, that is the craziest justification I have ever heard. Before we drag you down and book you, would you be willing to tell us whom you got your drugs from?"

"In the beginning it was Carl Grand. Later, it became Nathan Shankman."

"How did Grand convince you to become a pusher?"

"He showed me a video of him giving out drugs and selling them at a very cheap price. I knew he would easily get a hundred or so kids in a week if he wanted to. I saw it as a way to limit the number of kids. I know it sounds stupid, but I thought I was helping out."

"That's one of the lamest excuses I have ever heard for doing something illegal."

"There's something else he did. He showed up at my house one morning as I was leaving to school. He flashed his gun and said six words. 'Nice house, nice kids, nice wife.' I had no doubt that he would kill them if I did not cooperate. I had to make a choice and I chose my family. I know the other stuff about making sure that fewer kids would get addicted is crap."

"Would you be willing to testify against Shankman? It would look good to the sentencing judge."

"Sure, Detective. I'm ashamed. My wife doesn't know. My kids won't understand."

"And would you be willing to testify for the three young men who were your sales force that you seduced them with promises of helping their families get loans for down payments on homes?"

"No problem, Detective."

"And could you give us any clues as to who Shankman or Grand were getting their drugs from?"

"Sorry, Detective. I only dealt with those two."

"Pat, we need to get back to the drawing board. We've got three corpses with one suspect for only one of them. We have no idea who killed the pharmacist and no idea who killed the Barnes kid. We uncovered a drug-dealing scheme with a principal in charge but no idea who was above the guy he was dealing with. It seems simple and we could put a ribbon on the case. We could say 'unknown assailant murders woman' and stick it in the unsolved murders file. Aside from working something out for the three kids, taking Shankman to jail, and getting Edwards into court, our work could be over."

"The fact that your talking like that, boss, makes me think you don't think it's over."

"I don't. The pharmacist's murder can't be a coincidence. Somehow, I think she's got to be the key. The other corpse may also be critical."

"The only folks connected to the pharmacist are the attorney, the parents, and her brother. We need to go back to them. I think we should start with the parents, boss."

"I agree, Pat. We also need to check the last address for the father of the Lopez woman."

The toothpick was out, and Zuma was humming.

"I know that one, boss. I know the version by U2, and it applies perfectly. It's 'I Still Haven't Found What I'm Looking For.' I like it, boss, when I can guess the tune that applies to what we are trying to deal with and figure out. It makes the cases seem lighter. They seem less gruesome and burdensome."

"I know, Pat. We deal with the worst of the worst. Thieves, murder, pedophiles, and child killers, and it gets to lots of police officers. We have high rates of suicide, divorce, and burnout. I find, like you, that being able to frame the stuff with a song capturing the similarity between the reality and a movie makes it less burdensome. It doesn't make me forget but helps me think about it differently."

"Speaking of differently, I spoke with my neighbor."

"How did that go? Did the kindness routine work? What act of kindness did you come up with?"

I knocked on his door, and he looked through the peephole and didn't open the door and just asked what the hell did I want now. I told him that I was wrong to ask him to lower his music. He had a perfect right to play what he wanted and how he wanted to listen to it, and I wanted to apologize. He got quiet and for a few moments I thought that would be the end. He finally opened the door. He's a real big guy and he looked at me suspiciously. He was not afraid. I told him I was sorry, and I asked him if there was something I could do to show him that I was not upset and wanted to be a good neighbor. When he asked me what I meant by doing something? I repeated the things we had mentioned. He hesitated quite a bit and finally asked if I could pick up bottle of Jack Daniels once a week and a carton of Camels. I said that would not be a problem. I told him he didn't have to pay in advance, and I would leave the receipts in his mailbox and when he had a chance, he could reimburse me. I asked him when he would like to start and he said, right away would be fine. I got the stuff, came back in a half hour, knocked on his door, and he said thank you. I left quickly saying I had to go to work."

"What happened to the music, Pat?"

"What music, boss? What are you talking about?"

Zuma roared with laughter. "I can't wait to tell, Claudia. There's a great song with the words that have the line, 'Killing me softly with his words.' You did it, Pat Vasquez, with words and deeds. Congratulations. You're already a great cop and now you're a great neighbor."

CHAPTER 11

"Boss, last night I got a call from our proud, 'I'm one of the most knowledgeable and proudest Chicanas in the world.'"

"I knew she couldn't wait to get her hands on you, Pat. I'm hoping you were professional."

"It wasn't a problem, boss. She called because she had received a letter from her dad. It was posted two days after his body was dumped into the ocean. I asked her to read it to me and she was willing. I also asked her to take a picture of it and send it to our office. She agreed."

"What do you remember her saying, Pat?"

Pat relayed the contents of the letter as he remembered it to Zuma. "Mr. Lopez said that he had an agreement with his supplier to not go into the schools with high percentages of Mexican or Central American kids. It looked like this agreement was going to be broken when Carl Grand told him that he was expanding the business. The supplier to Grand and Lopez didn't like the breaking of the agreement, and he was going to meet with Mr. Lopez and Mr. Grand and talk Grand out of it. Her dad said that he knew that might not work and if something happened to him, he wanted police to be informed about Grand and the big boss whose name was Abraham Nassar. She also gave me an address. Her dad gave the letter to a friend and said if he didn't hear from him in two days, he should send the letter. Her dad said that Grand had accidentally told him that he had killed the pharmacist. Grand had gotten pissed off that a Jew, and a woman on top of it, was a big shot in the pharmacy. He began spewing all kinds of stuff about how blacks were still being screwed and the goddamn Jews were taking over and getting all the good jobs."

"Great work, Pat. How crazy is that? A black man selling drugs to black kids and sees the problem as not something he's doing but something that a white Jewish woman is doing. Some people never can look at themselves."

"You're right, boss. The proud Chicana is like that. I wonder if she'll ever change."

"Pat, the problem is that Grand is dead and so is her dad. We're only left with Nassar."

"I know, boss."

"Maybe Nassar felt the breaking of his rule and the squabbling between Lopez and Grand was too much. And maybe he was beginning to get tired of limiting sales and he saw the meeting as a way to get rid of the two of them and starting over."

"Could be, boss, but remember Grands' body and that of Mr. Lopez were found in the Pacific. How would Nassar handle two corpses? And there were two different caliber weapons used. Maybe Nassar had an accomplice?"

"I don't know, but I think that with a little more time we will figure that out. Pat, it's good that Carmela likes you and wanted you to know about her dad. How did you leave it with her?"

"I told her that as soon as we had further information that I would be calling."

I'll bet I know what song she was singing to herself after you hung up, Pat."

"Ok, boss, lay it out."

"It's a well-known song made famous by a group called The Doors, but I'm sure she is thinking of a different version by Jose Feliciano. I think you can guess what nationality he is. It's called "Light My Fire." Pat, she can't wait for you to set her night on fire. Let's go visit Mr. Abraham Nassar. He must be Egyptian. On the way over, I'd like to teach you a song that you can sing to Carmela to show her you are proud of being an American. It has American names like Martin and John but includes one from the Bible even though it's about an American."

"Boss, let's make this my last lesson in music or history this week."

"Sure, Pat. Last lesson. It's about four great Americans even though the title has only the three names of Abraham, Martin, and John. It goes like this."

Has anybody here seen my old friend Abraham?
Can you tell me where he's gone?
He freed a lotta people, but it seems the good die young
But I just looked around and he's gone.
Has anybody here seen my old friend John?
Can you tell me where he's gone?
He freed a lotta people, but it seems the good die young
But I just looked around and he's gone.
Has anybody here seen my old friend Martin?
Can you tell me where he's gone?
He freed a lotta people, but it seems the good die young
But I just looked around and he's gone.
Didn't you love the things they stood for?
Didn't they try to find some good for you and me?
And we'll be free,
Someday soon it's gonna be one day.
Has anybody here seen my old friend Bobby?
Can you tell me where he's gone?
I thought I saw him walkin' up over the hill
with Abraham, Martin and John.

"So, that's Abraham Lincoln, Martin Luther King, Jr., John and Bobby Kennedy, right?"

"Right, Pat. All great Americans and we, as the song urges, should love the things they stood for. It's something you should get Carmela to listen to. Show her that there are other things she could also be proud of."

"Thanks, boss, that might be fun. It will certainly be challenging. That's a good one. It will probably be provocative for her and is a demanding one for me."

CHAPTER 12

Abraham Nassar's four-bedroom apartment was on the 14th floor of a high-rise building at the end of San Vincente Boulevard in Santa Monica with a view of the Pacific Ocean. Nassar towered over the six-foot Lopez and the six-foot-two Carl Grand. After inviting them both to move to his office and sit on two chairs facing each other, he asked them if the squabble between the two of them involving the increase in selling to schools in heavily populated Mexican communities could be resolved. Lopez was against it and was adamant. Grand was just as adamant and kept talking about profits and how others were already selling and profiting in the Mexican schools.

"But it's not me, Carl, or someone I know."

"You could use the extra money and give scholarships."

"Good thinking, Carl. Destroy ten kids to give one kid a scholarship. Pretty fucking dumb."

"Don't call me dumb you fucking border-crossing wetback."

"It's dumb reasoning. Carl. But more importantly, you broke my rule. You never checked with me. You decided to do something outside our agreement. You had to figure I wouldn't like that. If you didn't know that I wouldn't agree, maybe Lopez is right, you are dumb. And you were really dumb when you got pissed off at a pharmacist and killed her with the possibility of drawing more attention to you and to possibly me."

Grand dropped his jaw, and before he could respond, Nassar deftly pulled a pistol from his open drawer and shot Grand twice in the heart. The blood spattered out of Grand's heart all over the chair and rug. Lopez clenched and thought he was next. Nassar saw the tightening and reassured Lopez he was safe.

"Please, do not worry. You are a good and loyal employee. Grand was stupid and a bigot. I don't want people like that working for me. I will need your help to wipe up this mess of blood and to get his body out of here. We can take it down in the elevator to my van and dump it into the Pacific. We will need to use the carpet to roll his body into since I have no use for it anymore. Let's use a plastic bag over the corpse. We need to wait until dark and low tide. I can drive the van onto the beach and dump it right near the pier."

After edging the van just under the pier and taking the corpse out of the plastic bag, Lopez and Nassar waded out twenty yards to make sure the body was covered by water. They knew the tide would carry it out. They left the blanket on shore, knowing that hobos would pick it up and use it for sleeping. The blood would not bother them.

"Mr. Lopez, I'd like to call you Daniel. You have been an excellent and loyal employee. I would like to give you or your daughter some extra money as a gift."

Daniel Lopez became wary. He did not want Nassar to have anything to do with his daughter and certainly not to know where his daughter lived.

Thank you, Mr. Nassar. No need for anything extra. I appreciate the thought and am just glad that we will be able to continue our arrangement."

"Not exactly."

And with those words Nassar took out his revolver and shot Lopez in the head. It was a bit of a struggle carrying out the body. Fortunately for Nassar, Daniel Lopez weighed fifty pounds less than Carl Grand.

CHAPTER 13

Of the many things Joe Zuma loved about Santa Monica, walks along the ocean in the early morning hours were his most enjoyable. He loved the diversity of the city, its efforts to keep rent control, and the different upscale and family-priced restaurants along with their different ethnic offerings of foods as well as the new modern high rises along with the old bungalows. But the walks before the sun came up were his favorite. He would get up before Claudia and the sun rose and watch the sun slowly rising in the east to brighten the sky over the ocean and say hello to the dog lovers who brought their animals to frolic before the lifeguard showed up and ticketed them. He smiled, knowing that they were all violating some municipal code about dogs off a leash and swimming, but he did not mind. He made sure that his gun and his badge could not be seen. It was peaceful and quiet, and he could almost meditate. Even though he had to have his phone with him to be on call, he could still relax. When he got back, he would take coffee for Claudia and bring it to her in bed. None of the stresses at work or crimes he was involved with solving interfered with this routine, which he was able to do at least once a week.

One of the regulars who he passed each time he walked had begun to first smile and then say hello and one day asked him if he had a dog and if not what kind of work he did. Joe smiled and said he did not own any animals and that he worked for the city. The man said, "How lucky we are to have this in our backyard." Zuma smiled and agreed but kept walking. He did not want to develop a closer relationship with this other regular. Zuma also brought ten singles with him every time he went on his walk, and when he passed someone sleeping in a tent or on a bedroll, he would drop a couple of bucks on their sleeping gear. On this morning, when he was dropping the money a woman jumped up and said she knew that he had been doing this and wanted to thank him. "I also know you are with the police, 'cause I've seen you on TV." Zuma smiled and said he would appreciate her keeping her information to herself and that they would have a secret. She smiled and wished him a good day. Zuma headed back home, thinking that a bit of kindness toward the downtrodden goes a long way. He told Claudia the story of the woman and her recognition as he brought her the coffee in bed. She smiled and said she knew how famous he was getting to be because she had noticed all the people who stared at him when they were dining out.

On the way to the office, Zuma thought about the dogs frolicking in the ocean and retrieving the sticks that their owners had cast out and how the animals are never tired of that, how the hobos are never tired of sleeping on the beach, and how he is never tired of his walks. Animals and humans must like repetition. His final thought just before he was going to speak to Pat was about the contact with the woman who recognized him. He hoped that there would be no repetition of their encounter.

"Pat, this is what we've got. We think Nassar killed Carl Grand and Daniel Lopez either alone or with an accomplice. Grand, because he was a bigot and anti-Semitic, got pissed off and killed Shankman. Maybe Grand killed Lopez when he realized that he shouldn't have said anything about his killing Shankman. He may have been worried that Lopez would go back to Nassar because he was a witness to Grand's murder. That might explain the different caliber bullets. Right now, we still don't know who killed Thomas Barnes and what are we going to do with the damn principal or with Nathan Shankman. I think we need to visit Mr. Nassar. There is a fairly unknown song, Pat, about the sounds that animals like dogs, cats, and mice make. The song says, "However, no one knows the sound that the fox makes. So, let's go hear what the fox says."

"Sure, boss, thanks for not singing."

Zuma rang the buzzer, and when he announced that he would like to come up and visit, Nassar said he had been expecting a visit.

"Come in, gentlemen. Can I offer you a drink or perhaps something to eat? I wondered how long it would be before you visited me. Let's go into my office."

Zuma and Pat walked past the spacious living room, with its majestic view of the Pacific into the study, which was full of sports and music memorabilia. Nassar was in all of the pictures of former Lakers, Kobe Bryant and Shaquille O'Neill, as well as owner Jerry Buss. Zuma knew that two pictures must have just been added: one was of Kobe and his daughter Gianna and the other one was a shot showing all the seats at the STAPLES Center covered with the Bryant jersey. There were lots of pictures of Motown groups: The Supremes, The Temptations, and Gladys Knight and the Pips with Nassar posing in each one. A separate photograph of Barry Gordy along with Nassar was framed in gold with a "Thank you Abraham" signed by Gordy. Zuma could barely tear himself away as Pat grew impatient.

"Do you love Motown only or do you love other music, Mr. Nassar?"

"I love famous and successful people. I admire them and they usually admire me. But I'm sure you are not here to discuss my tastes or heroes in music or sports."

"We certainly are not, Mr. Nassar. We are here to discuss your relationship to Carl Grand and Daniel Lopez."

"My accountant will be happy to provide you with any information about their earnings. They were my employees."

"What did they do for you."

"Anything and everything I wanted. Shopped, drove, collected rents. I own two large apartment buildings. Lopez and Grand were each assigned to a building. There's lots of stuff to do besides collect rents in a building of that size."

"And when was the last time you saw or spoke with your two employees?"

"I can't remember exactly. We did not speak often. Rents were delivered to my accountant. They took care of building stuff, tenant complaints, and fixing broken toilets and pipes. I made sure they wouldn't bother me with that kind of crap. All the records are with my accountant."

"Mr. Nassar, we have a letter indicating that Daniel Lopez was going to meet with you because you called him."

"That must have been when I needed to get some shopping done. He never showed up."

"He never showed up because his body was recovered near the Santa Monica pier. I'm sure you know the pier since you can see it from your living room window. And do you know that Carl Grand was also found near the pier."

"What can I tell you, Detective, I know nothing about how they were shot. But if you're going to continue this line of questioning, I will have to call my lawyer."

Zuma realized that Nassar had given up information that Zuma hadn't mentioned. He decided to not say anything also knowing that Nassar was too smart to not have realized that he had slipped.

"Mr. Nassar, do you own any guns? And if so, are they are registered?"

"I'll answer that question Detective Zuma and that will be the last one I answer. From now on, all your questions will be done with my lawyer present. I own two guns, and both are registered."

"And can you tell us their caliber?"

"As I said, Detective, I've answered your last question. If you want to ask more questions, I'll call my lawyer right now, and we can all meet down at your station. I'd like you to both leave now."

※

"You weren't exactly right, boss. The fox only made a few sounds but one that was damn important."

"He sure did, Pat. We need to get a warrant to search his place. I think he knows that we'll do that, and I'm sure the guns he said he has will be registered. But we need to search it anyway and I want to be in on it. Those pictures of the music groups were great. I counted over two dozen and I didn't have time to finish and I want to go back. There were a few I didn't recognize."

"Boss, please, no more music lessons for a while."

CHAPTER 14

As Zuma was leaving for work, Claudia mentioned that when she came home last night, she saw a homeless woman across the street sitting on the curb between two cars. "The woman smiled at me as if she knew me. I wonder if that is the one you befriended and who recognized you."

"If you see her again, Claudia, call me immediately. I don't want her coming around here. I thought she was going to be quiet with her recognition. I'll find out what she is up to. I don't think there is any need to worry but do call. I need to make a call now. I'll see you this evening. I'm not sure what time, but I will call you."

"Ms. Kouri, this is Detective Zuma. We need your help. Sorry to telephone you, but we have a lead on who might have killed your lover. We need a warrant to go through Mr. Abraham Nassar's apartment, and I would like to book him and have a trial if possible."

"I need something more than a suspicion. What more can you tell me?"

"He had two men who worked for him who were murdered. We have a letter from one of them written to his daughter saying that if she didn't hear from him that he probably was knocked off by Nassar."

"A letter from a deceased is never good evidence, Detective. There are no witnesses. It won't get you a conviction. I need something more."

"I am not concerned if I don't get a conviction. I want publicity. This guy is well known in the sports and music worlds. He undoubtedly has, in the course of his career, made some enemies.

Someone might come forward now if they see his name. All of the people I'm thinking of are older and probably would not be too worried about retaliation."

"I'll get the warrant for you. I'll have to convince my boss about a trial. Knowing you're going to lose is not something he likes to do. It's expensive for the taxpayers."

"So, is getting kids addicted who cost taxpayers for rehab, prisons, or stealing to support their habit?"

"It'll be a long shot, but I'll try. It's the least I can do for Phyllis."

"I have another thought. Can you check on the guy who owned two buildings? Can you find out if there were any violations?"

"No problem, Detective. Lila, can you go run down the hall to Building and Safety and tell Carlos that I need a favor and see if he can pull the inspection reports for these two buildings? Detective, this should only take a few minutes."

Lila returns.

"This is really weird. One building is clean as a whistle. The other has lots of violations."

"My guess, Ms. Kouri is that the clean building was handled by Daniel Lopez and the one with violations was handled by Carl Grand. There were mostly Mexicans renting in both buildings. Why would there be a difference? We're pretty sure that Grand was a stone cold racist, even towards his own. I'm sure he would not want to be helpful to people he despised. Can we use those violations to bring charges against Nassar? That would get some publicity."

"Those are charges my boss would go for, rather than that letter. He's liberal and like me, he doesn't like seeing people with less means getting screwed over. I'll speak to him right now along with my asking for a warrant. I'll get that for you in ten minutes. Even if he is busy, he'll be glad to get this out."

"Pat, let's get two men over to Nassar's building—one to stay in the garage and the other at the front door. I'm going to call him and give him some time just to see if he tries to leave with anything he might be wanting to hide."

When Zuma and Pat arrived, Nassar and his lawyer, Ira Beck, were there. The lawyer asked to see the warrant. Zuma said they just wanted access to the safe to look for guns and records from his rental buildings but were not going to give the place a thorough search. Pat waited for Nassar to open the safe, and Zuma wandered into the office with all the photos. He sat gazing at all the pics and looked and thought and started to speak to them.

"Come on, you wonderful artists. You have brought so much fun and joy to people. Do one more good thing."

It hit him like a rock. If he put an S for the Supremes, a W for Stevie Wonder, and I for the Isley Brothers, an F for the Four Tops, and a T for the Temptations, it spelled SWIFT. He began to laugh. He started to play with the other artists and quickly came up with D for Diana Ross, I again for Isley and G for Gladys Knight and thought DIG. "Yes, Mr. Nassar I'm sure that one of these wonderful people will come forth and dig up your past it should be swift for you from now on." As he was enjoying his playfulness, he noticed an address scrawled on a separate piece of paper next to the phone on Nassar's desk. He recognized it immediately.

"Boss, there were records from the rental business $20,000 in cash and two guns in the safe. They have the same caliber as we found on the victims. I will have to run a check on them."

"Mr. Nassar, I need to tell you your rights now before I handcuff you and book you for the attempted murders of Daniel Lopez, Carl Grand, and Thomas Barnes. We're also going to charge you with a set of building code violations. You're going to have to account for that sum of cash."

"Ira, get the goddamn bail money ready and meet me at the police station. He has no hard evidence for anything. I'm not worried. I'll plead guilty to…"

"Abraham, shut up. You've already said too much. Do not say anything more to anyone. I'll meet you at the station with bail money."

"Boss, how did you add Thomas Barnes into the list of vics?"

"Just took a gamble, Pat. I saw his name on Nassar's desk and couldn't imagine why he would know it. It couldn't be that he liked the kid. Nassar didn't like anyone unless they were famous. I knew it had to be something important and had nothing to lose. But let me tell you about the fun I had looking at the photographs again."

Zuma told him about the SWIFT and DIG creations and his hope that one of the SWIFTIES would come forth.

"I don't get why you think he would have enemies."

"Pat, all those photos were from people who were around or into drugs. I'm hoping some of them might be pissed off enough at what he did and see a chance to get back at him. A lot of lives were wrecked because of his supplying them with drugs. Sure, they were using but they were all young and they might see him now in a different light. I'm hoping they see him as having taken advantage of them. I'm hoping when someone sees his name or picture in the paper that there will be talk. And someone is bound to hear it on the grapevine. I think you must know that one, Pat."

"Yes, boss, I do. It is a very Gaye tune about jealousy and loss and getting bad news through gossip."

"Pat, it's getting to be harder and harder to teach you more."

"Yeah, boss, you'll be out of the music teacher's role pretty soon, but I think I will still need you for movies."

"Well, since you do let's get to the precinct and book Mr. Nassar."

On the way out of the high rise, Zuma spotted the woman who had recognized him on the beach.

"I don't appreciate your hanging out in front of my home and would like you to stop doing that."

"I'm sorry, Detective, I want to make my keen powers of observation work for me and I think the local paper might be interested in your habit of running in the morning and your local residence. You fame is nothing you can run away from. I thought I'd make a little money by letting the public know more about their famous detective."

Zuma felt his anger rise. He stared hard at the woman and reached into his wallet. "Sorry, you decided to put an end to our relationship." He decided to shove his wallet back into his rear pocket. "Have a nice day and I'll see you on the beach." He turned before the woman could respond grabbed Pat on the arm and headed towards his police car.

"What was that, boss?"

"I'm not sure, Pat. I guess killing them with kindness doesn't always work."

CHAPTER 15

After fingerprinting Nassar, taking his picture, and locking him up, Ira Beck was in court asking that Nassar be released.

"He is an honorable citizen, your honor. He has no criminal record. These charges of murder are based on a letter from a dead person. There are building code violations but I'm sure that my client did not know about them. He had a manager who was unresponsive to tenants. His other building has zero violations."

"Do you object, Detective Zuma?"

"Yes, we do, your honor. Mr. Nassar has lots of money, and I'm sure leaving the country and not returning would be an option for him. At minimum, we would need his passports."

"I'll accept those terms, your honor. How can I get my client released immediately?"

On the way out of the courtroom, Nassar walked up to Zuma. "I'll see you in court, Detective Zuma. With my Jewish lawyer defending me, an Egyptian, I don't think you will get a jury to do anything to me. I think the papers are going to have a heyday with your office prosecuting an upright Arab-looking citizen. The Arab community is going to have a heyday seeing what your office is doing as his harassment. And when they see a Jew defending me, I know you will have lost your case before it even starts."

"Boss, that guy is as smug and cocky as they come."

"We'll see how cocky he remains when his picture is in the paper and hopefully one of the SWIFTIES will call and want to talk to us. We will need to steer him or her towards an interview. Call your friend at the newspaper, Pat, and get her ready. We also need to put a tail on Nassar and get some security ready to protect the Motown hero who comes forward.

"Boss, it's more likely to be a heroine."

"Pat, Nassar seems determined to get rid of any persons who knew he was connected to drugs. That's why I think Barnes was killed. That leaves Nathan Shankman, but he may think the principal also knew him. We need to get some protection for the two of them."

"I'll set that up, boss. Whoops, here's a call from Ms. Chicana of the West Coast and Beyond.

"Hi, Carmela. What? You didn't tell me that there was also a key in the envelop and now you are afraid to go down to Union Station and open the box? And you want me to go with you? Wait a moment. I'll have to speak to my boss. No, Carmela, I'm not being a good, little Mexican boy. I have to speak with him. I can only meet you if it's part of our investigation, and he's here right now, so I can ask him. He's nodding yes."

"Pat, go. There may be something in the box related to our case and you'll be there when she opens it, so she won't be able to hide anything. There's a song her father might have sung when he sent her the key. My favorite version is by the Beatles."

"Boss, I thought I was catching up to you."

"You're catching up, Pat, but you have a bit of a way to go. It's called 'You've Got to Hide Your Love Away.' Maybe her dad had to hide some of his love from his one and only daughter."

"I'm leaving, boss. Too many songs and groups. I'll keep you posted on what I find in the box.

"Carmela, I'll meet you at Union Station. You've never been there? Yes, it's pretty big. Let's meet in front of the sign that says, 'To Trains.' Don't worry. You have my cell and I have yours in case you get lost."

Pat was surprised at how anxious Carmela sounded. He wondered if it was about the contents of the box, hearing from her father again, or was it simply not knowing her way around. He would soon find out.

When Carmela saw Pat, she started to tear up.

"I don't know why I'm so scared. I thought my father had told me everything. I thought we never kept secrets. Now, I'm afraid to find something about him that would make me feel differently towards him. Pat, I don't want to know anything about his fishy business. I needed you to come. Even though I've called you weak, I know you are stronger than I am. Please promise me that if the note you read is about illegal stuff you won't tell me. I don't want to know. Please, promise me, Pat. You keep it and use it. Maybe it can help you, but I don't want to know."

Carmela was sobbing deeply. Pat put his arms around her and whispered softly.

"You have my word. Give me the key and let's go. I'll open the box. You can stand back."

"Carmela, you have nothing to worry. It's money and lots of it. A note that is in Spanish which even I can translate It says 'te quiero. Papa.'"

"Thank you, thank you, Pat. Thank you, God, and thank you, Papa."

"And it looks like over $20,000. It's in hundred-dollar bills. It's all yours and you can count it."

"Not here, Pat. Please come back with me so I can count it. I promise you I won't ask you to stay. I'll just ask you to accompany me to the bank so I can deposit it."

"There's a police office here in the station. Let's go there and you can count it, and then I'll take you to your bank."

—⟋⟍—

"Boss, nothing about our case. Her papa left her a lot of money. She's counting it right now, and I'm going to take her to the bank when she is through. She was not the cocky babe she has pretended to be. She really broke down when she realized what the gift her father had given her was all about."

"Pat, I think we can rule her out as a suspect so maybe…maybe you can…"

"Thanks for looking out for me, boss. I'm going to be patient with this situation. There is a song you taught me. It was one of your favorites, came from a movie called *The Umbrellas of Cherbourg*. The lines go like this: 'If it takes forever, I will wait for you; for a thousand summers, I will wait for you.'"

"Pat, something is coming over you. You're getting to be a real romantic."

"Your influence again, boss! I remember that you told me you sometimes sang it to Claudia."

CHAPTER 16

Avril Kouri's boss was happy bringing Abraham Nassar to trial for rent violations. It got the publicity that Zuma was hoping for. During the trial and before a verdict was handed down, Nassar offered to pay the $25,000 in rent violations and set up a special fund for all the tenants that had to see a doctor or go to the hospital for any illness contracted because of the cold weather and not having heat in the building. He pleaded no contest to the judgment of guilt and was fined $50,000.

The story in the newspaper resulted in a phone call to the paper from one of the Pips who had sung with Gladys Knight. The Pip gave an interview saying how he was seventeen when Nassar had introduced him to drugs. He had seen him do this to many other young singers and assumed that this was normal, and everything would be fine. His addiction had cost him many lost years in rehab, and he wanted the world to know that Nassar was a predator. That story resulted in several others calling the paper and telling their story. The sales of the local newspapers soared. It was exactly what Zuma had hoped for. As expected, the call came.

"Detective Zuma, I can't stop the newspaper from defaming me. My offer of medical bill payments has not stopped the stories. I know that you were behind this, but I'd like you to listen to my idea of how you can help me stop it or at least minimize it. I think that you would benefit."

"I'm listening."

"What if I gave a million dollars to a rehab center that specializes in artists and another million to support high school performers in public schools. The money could be used for the kids to buy and own their own instrument and a stipend every month for their high school career. You would announce this with me at your side, along with the district attorney, and I will apologize for having inflicted harm and hoping this is a form of reparations."

"I can do that for you but only if you indicate your connections to the murders of Shankman, Lopez, Grand, and the Barnes kid. And, along with that you, tell us about your connection to Mr. Tapper and Nathan Shankman."

"I will agree to that. I can even tell you now that I never met Tapper and only knew that Shankman was working for Grand. But first, I want to be able to stand in front of the press with you and the DA. After that, I will talk about what I know concerning the four murders."

Right after his public announcement, Zuma asked Nassar to come down to the precinct and tell him what he knew about the four murders. Nassar indicated that he would show up next morning with his lawyer. When Nassar did not show up, Zuma called and got no answer. He and Pat went to the apartment and found Abraham Nassar on the floor. He was dead and had been shot with two bullets in his heart.

"Pat, we now have five murders. Who is left that is connected to all of these vics?"

"Both sets of parents make four. Then, there is Avril Kouri, Mr. Tapper, and Nathan Shankman, and that makes seven, boss."

"You left out one, Pat."

"Who's that?"

"You left out Carmela."

CHAPTER 17

There were seven names on the board.

"Pat, I know you think that Carmela didn't have anything to do with killing Nassar, but she had motive. The note from her father made it clear to her that it was Nassar who killed her dad. We have a body and all we need is a weapon."

"Look, boss, I know I have feelings for Carmela but she's not the kind of woman who would murder. I just can't think of her in that way."

"That's why there is a saying that love is blind. Unfortunately, Pat, given the right circumstances, any of us can murder."

"Boss, even if she were guilty, what would we gain? Isn't this like that situation where Claudia convinced you not to go after the person you thought was guilty? If she did kill Nassar, we both know he was a really bad guy. If we go after Carmela, her life will be ruined."

"Sorry, Pat, I don't see it that way. If you want to pull out of this investigation, I will understand and that will be okay with me."

No, boss, I'll stay on it. I'm not afraid to pursue finding the murderer because I know that Carmela would not have killed Grand."

"The other names on the board who had motive would be: the Shankmans, revenge for the murder of their daughter; Nathan, for his sister's murder; Avril, revenge for the loss of her lover; and Tapper, whose motive could be for threatening him and his family and ruining his career. So, we have motives for all seven, Pat, lets run a check for registered weapons and make a visit to see if any of them own weapons. Let's check all the weapons you find with the caliber of shots found in the vics."

It took Pat along with two colleagues one day to do the interviews. He felt very uncomfortable about interviewing Carmela, so he asked his assistant, Manuel, to do it. Nathan, Avril, Carmella, and Mrs. Mimi Shankman were willing to have samples of the markings on the fired bullet compared to the markings on their own weapons. None had similar marking to the bullets that had killed Nassar.

Mimi Shankman showed up in Zuma's office and declared that she had murdered Nassar.

Zuma was suspicious. She had motive but her weapon had no markings.

"Mrs. Mimi Shankman, I want to tell you that based on your confession we are going to have to charge you with the murder of Abraham Nassar, but I find it hard to believe you. Where did you get the weapon? Where did you learn to shoot? I need to inform you that you have the right to…"

"Thank you, Detective Zuma. I've already asked Avril Kouri to represent me."

"She can't defend you. She is a prosecutor."

"I asked her a few days ago to represent me when I knew I would need one. She resigned and agreed. I learned a lot from following Nassar's trial. I will have an orthodox Muslim woman defending me, an Orthodox Jew female. If there are any women in the jury pool, I'm sure they will be sympathetic towards a woman who was trying to avenge her daughter's murder."

"You're probably right, Mrs. Shankman. Make your phone call."

Avril Kouri never asked Mimi if she actually killed Nassar but was impressed with the diligence and carefulness that her client had gone about in preparing to either commit her crime or make it look like she had committed the crime. It reminded her of the way Maddie had prepared for her day's work. When Mimi saw that Nassar had trouble with one of his buildings, she made up a business card, registered the business as a cleaning business and showed up at Nassar's apartment seeking employment. Security refused to let her in, but she waited and waited and finally her patience was rewarded. Her pitch to Nassar was that it would look very good to his clients if he replaced his manager with a woman who would be able to express sympathy and understanding to the women in the building who had to care for their children. She had taken an intensive Spanish language course and would be able to converse with them. The male tenants would not be anxious, feeling that a woman would not be threatening to them, and they could outtalk her for late rent. She would deliver rent to his apartment twice a month. At first, he didn't not want her to come and work in his building, but she convinced him that it might be good PR for him to be seen as employing a Jew and a woman. Her statement to the court was direct and appealed to the women jurors.

"I've done something and am doing something that will honor my daughter. I don't have many years left, but at least my daughter will know I stood up for her even though I had to break the law. It is also for my son. He should learn to stand up for what is right and not continue to look for quick and easy fixes."

"I also have done something and am doing something that will honor my lover."

The trial did not take long. Avril felt that by defending her lover's mother, she was also honoring her deceased lover. Avril never challenged the shooting of Nassar but sought to paint Nassar as a predator and evil person and Mrs. Shankman as a woman heartbroken with the loss of her daughter and angry at the justice system. Avril could see that her arguments about a mother's loss and the unfairness of the justice system were resonating to the women on the jury panel and to the two males of color. In an unprecedented case, the jury returned a verdict of justifiable homicide. The sentencing judge assigned Mrs. Shankman to one year in jail, three years' probation, and a fine. Avril had noticed during the trial Mr. Shankman had never appeared. He did show up at the sentencing and the judge allowed him to say goodbye to his wife. Avril thought she saw tenderness in the man. Nathan, who had been there for both days, stood up and saluted his mother as she was taken away. Avril asked the guards if she could have a moment with her client in a secluded office, next to the judge's chambers.

CHAPTER 18

"I called you in here because I have a private issue I want to discuss. It's important and I think I have thought it through pretty carefully, but I need your guidance. I'm the outsider in this, and you know a lot more than I do."

Mrs. Shankman sat with disbelief. How could this well-educated successful lawyer believe that she could be helpful? Especially now that she was going off to jail. She started to suggest that she could not be helpful in any way and that Avril was wasting her time but was cut off.

"I'm planning to make you a grandmother."

"What are you talking about? Are you crazy? That's preposterous. My daughter is dead."

"Of course, I know that. But this is what your daughter and I planned. We were saving money to get a house before we had a child but decided it would be better if we could harvest our eggs before we got older. We both had our eggs frozen. I can look for a sperm bank, which has a good reputation, and I can have Marilyn's eggs impregnated. These fertilized eggs can be checked for their health and vitality, and I can have one or more placed in my uterus. Everything goes forward then just like a normal pregnancy."

"Avril, are you saying you will raise this child Jewish?"

"I'm saying that the eggs come from a Jewish woman and you will have a grandchild whom you can visit and teach them about your holidays, your prayers, your music, and your games. I will do the same. I will expose him or her to our holidays, prayers, and music. If there is anything I learned by loving your daughter, it was the benefits of learning about differences.

"The child will get equal exposure. I will feel better if you are around to teach her or him the things Marilyn would have wanted him or her to learn. My only requirement for you is that you do not bring him or her up in an orthodox temple."

"Won't it make him or her crazy to come to my home for Judaism and your home with Muslim practices?"

"I don't think so. Children can understand if we explain things. When they are young, they respond to food, music, games, and hugs. You and I can make sure he or she has lots of that. As he or she gets older and asks questions, we will tell the truth. There will be no secrets."

"I'm not sure how my husband will feel about all this. Once he knows the child has a Jewish mother, and it is Marilyn's eggs, he will probably want to take it away from you."

"I'm a smart lawyer. That will not happen. He might put restrictions on your visits. I don't want my child around your husband. I know enough about him through Marilyn."

"If he sees me raising the child in a nonorthodox temple, he will be furious. If I have to leave him so I can love my grandchild, I will. Bless you, Avril. You are a wonderful daughter-in-law."

"And you will be a marvelous grandmother. Let's not tell Nathan till I am in the sixth month. I want to make sure that all is well. If there is a bris, I will make sure you get out of jail for the ceremony. You may be out even when I am delivering. You will miss very little time."

"I know Nathan will be a wonderful uncle. It may even straighten him out."

"Time's up, ladies. You need to say your goodbyes."

CHAPTER 19

Neither Zuma nor Pat were convinced that Mimi Shankman had killed Abraham Nassar. Despite the evidence that she had a motive and there was a body and had taken gun shooting training, the weapon did not have the markings. In the trial, she said that she had gotten rid of the gun she used in the murder and by throwing it off the pier during high tide and had bought a second gun that she felt she might need for protection since there had been a number of break-ins in her neighborhood. Zuma did not want to put the file on the murder of Abraham Nasser into the "solved box."

The trial of Mr. Carl Edwards lasted three days. Zuma had written a letter indicating the high level of cooperation the principal had given to the solution of the cases. The verdict of guilty came back with a recommended maximum sentence of five years in jail. The defense attorney was Avril Kouri who, in this her second trial as a criminal defense lawyer, came up with a proposal that she presented to the judge before he was deciding on sentencing. Her proposal was that the principal be allowed to show up at the middle school five days a week, be returned to jail in the evening, and that he would work with the ten most difficult students in each teacher's class. He would get to know their names and family issue but still make it an academic relationship. If at the end of the first semester there had been no improvement in academic and behavioral measures, he would continue to serve the rest of his sentence in jail. If there was improvement, he would work at the school for the five years in the same capacity. In that way, all the entering students at the high school would have some tutoring from the start. The proposal also suggested that if there was an improvement, the defendant be allowed to serve the remaining time while living at home and reporting once a month to his probation officer.

The judge liked the proposal and Avril won her second case. When Nathan got word of the sentence, he decided to show up at Avril's office.

"I want to make my mother proud and do something to honor my sister. I am here to tell you I did sell drugs. Here is my weapon. I never used it to shoot anyone. I would like you to see if we can get the same sentence as Tapper."

"Good for you, Nathan. I know your sister would have been proud of you for doing this. Maybe from where she is now, she will be proud. I'm going to speak to my old boss and see if we can negotiate this without a trial. It will save the county money. I just need to make sure that Zuma is not going to press charges. We probably have to pick a different school, but I think my boss would be happy to make an announcement of how he is saving money and getting criminals to do good."

"This was quite a case, boss—four dead, two with guilty sentences, and one admitting guilt who got a plea bargain. We did well."

"Yes, and two of those sentenced will be doing good things for the community. I wish more criminal cases could be adjudicated that way."

"We also got an ally who's a criminal defense attorney, boss. That is quite unusual and a big benefit to us for future work."

"Speaking of future, what is going on with you and Carmela? Have you two been seeing each other?"

"Yes, boss, we have, but I'm not sure what I want to do."

"I know the perfect person for you to speak with. Let's meet Claudia for dinner."

CHAPTER 20

Zuma and Claudia were alone as Pat said he would be running late.

"Let's order first. Claudia, I told Pat you are the best person in the world to give relationship advice."

"Joe, darling, I don't give advice. I just listen. I want you to listen. That woman hobo is still coming around and I'm scared."

"I didn't tell you, Claudia, but she showed up and wanted me to give her money for not going to the papers. I told her she could do whatever she wanted. I was not going to be threatened by her."

But Joe, I am. Remember that experience I had with the hobo I found so interesting that I painted his portrait and who turned out to be a robber and a murderer? I'm afraid, Joe."

Zuma was perplexed. He had no problem understanding Claudia's fear but why would this woman keep coming around to harass Claudia? What did she have to gain? Was she trying to send a message to Zuma?

"Claudia, I understand that you are frightened and worried but there is nothing I can do. She is not violating any major ordinances that I can have her picked up for. At most, it could be for loitering, but she would be out a in a few days. If I do it again there would be a suit. The woman seemed pretty savvy to me."

"I can't believe that you as the chief detective of our police department can't figure out a way to make me, your wife, feel safe."

Zuma had only heard this degree of hurt anger when Claudia had been arguing with Zuma not to arrest the woman suspect that he was convinced had killed her husband.

"Okay, Claudia. I'll pick her up and speak with her and try and find out what she wants."

"No, Joe. Try is not good enough. I want her to stop. I want to feel safe. I expect you to help."

Zuma sat nodding his head as if to say he understood and would do it. At that moment, Pat came up to the table and Claudia switched into her sociable self.

"Hi, Pat. Joe has told me a little about the issues you are having with Carmela. You can tell me only what you feel comfortable sharing."

It took a few moments as Pat began clicking his tongue against his gums.

"I feel pretty crazy about Carmela, Claudia. I admire her ambition, intelligence, and sensitivity to others. It doesn't hurt that her father left her some money, so she is comfortable, and the new store is doing well. I like that she is happy in her work. She has not been depressed about the loss of her father nor is she ashamed of what he did. She feels that what he did was done in order to help her and that was the best he could do as a father and as an uneducated Latino. She respects my work. She's not too keen on my lack of Latino knowledge but she sees that I am willing to learn. And she likes to learn also. Joe helped me see what I could be proud of as an American, not just a Latino. And she listens to me."

"In the years I have worked with you, I have never heard you talk so much. You are really into her."

"I agree with Joe, Pat. Do you feel there is a problem?"

"I'm not sure I can stick out a marriage. I see too many guys on the force failing to keep their vows. I don't want to fail and hurt her."

"Pat, that sounds like love to me. And it also sounds like you're afraid of getting hurt."

"What do you mean?"

"I don't mean that you're thinking she might leave you. I mean, you're afraid to screw it up and experience the pain of your failing. You are protecting yourself."

"I see that, Claudia. Thank you."

"Pat, you know there is an old tune by Etta James, 'At Last My Love Has Come Along' or the more recent one by Nora Jones, 'Come Away with Me.'"

"Claudia, does Joe now have you doing what he does with songs?"

"I'm afraid he does, Pat. I'm trying to get him to do something else as well."

With these last words, Claudia looked at Zuma, and Pat saw Zuma's eyes. They were the eyes of a man who was confused and at the end of his patience.

CHAPTER 21

Zuma found the hobo lady on the beach as he was doing his walk. He was upset that his serene place had now been disturbed because of what she had been doing to his wife.

"Wake up. This is Officer Zuma. I need to speak with you. I can have you arrested for sleeping here, but I'd rather you tell me why you are harassing my wife."

"Good morning, Detective Zuma. I knew that by bothering her that you would get the message and try and do something. I wanted to speak with you where we could not be observed."

"I'm listening."

"I want you to vouch for me."

"Vouch? Vouch for what?"

"I want to rent the apartment that Nassar rented, and I need a reference. I've been living on this beach for three years and no one is going to accept my application unless I can show them some fairly recent residence or someone who can vouch for me. Your reputation would swing it for me."

Zuma thought quickly. Was this one of those homeless people who after living for years in the streets suddenly show up having saved thousands of dollars which they now felt secure enough to spend? Or was this connected to Nassar's murder? Was she connected to the drug schemes of Nassar and Grand? Did she murder Nassar? His head was spinning with the questions.

"And what if I refuse to vouch for you. What will you do?"

"Detective Zuma, you're already in some difficulty with people who believe that you have been harassing innocent Arab citizens. I can go to the press and show them how you hound the homeless. I have a recording of you waking me up this morning. That's harassment since you did not do it to others. I have pictures of you giving money to the other homeless who sleep on the beach. How do you think the citizens of Santa Monica will feel when they see their police supporting the homeless who are violating an ordinance instead of arresting them?"

Zuma was stumped. What would he have to lose if he vouched for her? It would look terrible for him if she turned out to be the killer of Nassar or involved with the drug selling schemes of Grand or Nassar. If he could even end up finding evidence for her guilt in either the murder or drug selling, would that balance the evidence that the defense attorneys would use about his vouching for her character? Even if she didn't have money to mount a good defense team, she would appeal to the public as an innocent homeless person who was doing no harm other than sleeping on the beach. On the other hand, he saw he could gain something.

"Will you stop harassing my wife? Do you promise to not show up at our home? Do you promise to disappear from her life?"

"Of course, I do, Detective. Now I have this paper that I would like you to sign. It indicates your understanding of my circumstances for not having a recent residence as well as your vouching for me as a woman of honesty and integrity and having the necessary resources for rent. Here is my bank account book which has over $100,000."

Zuma looked at the bank account book. He noticed her name and saw that the balance was $116,080. He was shocked. In turning the pages, he also noticed that there were regular monthly deposits for the past three years. This woman was involved in drug dealing, but he could at this point do nothing to pursue that. She would have been able to hire a pretty good defense lawyer.

"Here it is. You have my signature, and in exchange, I will assume I have your promise. If there is any further harassment, I will arrest you and investigate how you, a homeless person, made large monthly deposits."

"Thank you, Detective Zuma. I'm happy to reassure you that your wife will not be harassed and that you will not be hounded by the press for interviews about your treatment of the homeless. Have a good day. I won't be sleeping here much longer, so I will also say goodbye."

CHAPTER 22

Zuma was impressed. The woman had prepared the whole enactment from the beginning when she greeted him as he was dropping money on her bedroll to the harassment of his wife to taking advantage of the trial of Mrs. Shankman. All the while, she was planning to get what she wanted. This was one smooth operator. He wondered if, being so sharp, she could have been Nassar's connection. Maybe she was Nassar's boss and saw that he was now a liability and that she needed to get rid of him. He remembered the unsolved trial folder and knew that he was going to keep it open. He knew the name in the bankbook was different from the name of the woman he had vouched for. This made him realize that she was operating in the world with two identifies and her rental application, along with her bank book, would reveal a stable person with good monthly income rather than the homeless drug dealing woman he knew.

"Claudia, I took care of it. She will not be coming around anymore. You will not see her again."

"How did you do it, Joe?"

"I made a deal with her. I vouched for her being a responsible tenant in a rental application. She promised not to come around. I knew that these were just words from a clever conniver, so I told her that if she ever showed up at our home, I would investigate her. I could use as evidence what she had showed me in a bankbook. There were monthly deposits of large sums of money which I would guess were from drug dealing. She knew she would get busted. I also believe that she will not give up drug dealing, and she will get caught at some time in the future. I feel very confident, Claudia, that you will be safe."

"Thank you, Joe. I knew I could count on you. I'm glad you didn't do anything to hurt her."

"No, Claudia, I did not hurt her. The important thing is that I know and you feel safe."

Joe felt good in seeing Claudia relax. He felt less good knowing that a drug dealer was out there and that at this point he felt helpless about pursuing her. He knew he would have to speak with Pat.

"Boss, I could put a tail on her, and we could just try and catch her red-handed and a conviction would not be difficult. I could do everything to keep your name out of it so the press would not see you as the heavy."

"Pat, if she smells we are watching her, she will see it as a reason to break her promise and go to the press. Her appeal as a harassed homeless woman would get her lots of publicity and make one big headache for us. We have to be smarter than she is. We have to rely on knowing that her weak point is the likelihood that she will return to drug dealing. We have to be patient and wait a while. Right now, she is in the driver's seat with the controls firmly in her hands. We, at best, are spectators with lousy seats who can't see what is going on even though we know that drugs are probably still being distributed. And I don't have a song for that, Pat.

"There is only one thing that she did that involved an error and that we can do something about without her knowing. The name on the lease that I vouched for and the name on the bank booklet are not the same. One name is Alexandra Sherman, the other is Beatrice Yanotti. Let's see what you can come up with in running those names through every databank you can get hold of."

"Okay, boss. Running the two names through the fed and states should take some time, so it should take about a couple of weeks. By then, you may come up with a song."

CHAPTER 23

"Hi, boss, we got something! Alexandra Sherman was wanted for drug laundering in three states but with phone number and address unknown."

"That's the name on her bank book. If we freeze the account, she will know it's us. And she'll talk to the press. That's not going to help. Pat, did you find anything with the other name?"

"Yes, boss, but nothing illegal. Beatrice Yanotti had given up her child six years ago for adoption. There was a filing by a lawyer in Las Vegas."

"Pat, that is a great lead. Where is this lawyer located?"

"I've already checked that, boss. The problem is that he is dead, died just two years ago. Nothing suspicious. Was just old. He practiced in Nevada."

"Pack your bag, Pat. We may have to stay a few days to fight this bureaucracy and get access to the information. I'll tell Claudia, you tell Carmela. We need to leave early in the morning. Do you know which office we have to show up in? We don't have anything specific to show how Ms. Yanotti has been involved with drugs or murder. A judge is not likely to give us access to information just because we're suspicious. But we need to try."

"Boss, what are we going to do with the information if we get it? How will that help us?"

"Pat, I honestly don't know it will be useful. I just feel in my bones that we just have to have it. If we can talk to someone who knew her, they might be able to tell us something about Beatrice Yanotti that we don't know and that would help in getting a conviction other than the drug dealing that we know she is probably doing at this moment."

The encounters with the Nevada bureaucracy and the judge did prove fruitless. The judge would not accept the idea that regular and large monthly deposits were proof of any involvement in drug dealing and the two different signatures could mean that there were two different women. They decided to visit the address where the attorney who died had practiced. Someone was in and he indicated that he had taken over the practice of the prior tenant. It had been his father's practice. After explaining that they wanted to see if the names of the adopting parents, the attorney indicated that he could not do so and that it would be a violation of state law.

"Pat, I have one other ace up my sleeve. It's the kindness ace."

"Hello. Yes, this is Detective Zuma I want to speak to your chief, Captain Herman.

"Hi, Al, long time no speak. The last time we spoke about a year ago your daughter was graduating college and your son was starting. How are they doing? What? Your daughter has a job earning more than you. Isn't that wonderful. Congratulations. And how is Cindy doing now that your nest is emptying? A full-time job? That's great, the extra income must provide some relief for your son's education and your daughter's loans. Yes, Claudia and I are fine, thank you. Al, I need a favor. Is this a private phone? Okay, here's the favor. There's an attorney here in Vegas, nice guy, but he who won't let me see some old adoption papers. I was thinking you could ask him as you're local and most attorneys like to have good relations with the police. He might feel more disposed towards you than he was to me and would cooperate. Yes, I thought you would be able to do that. Pat Vasquez and I are on the way to the airport. Get back to me a ring when you know the names of any of the parties involved in the adoption. Do you have my phone number? Good. We'd like any names besides the mother, Beatrice Yanotti. It could be the fathers or the adopting parents' name. Thanks, Al. Really glad to hear your kids are doing so well and that you Cindy are also doing well. If the two of you have some time and want to come to LA, Claudia and I could put your up. Please feel free to invite yourself. You have a standing invitation. Thanks again, Al, for your help."

CHAPTER 24

"What was that about, boss?"

"I helped him out a while back. His wife was going nuts because her sister believed her husband was having an affair but couldn't prove anything. I was able to track down the guy on a number or his trysts in Santa Monica and gave the evidence to Al. His wife was able to help her sister get a big settlement since the guy was a politico and did not want any publicity."

"There's your help and kindness rap again, boss."

Zuma heard the phone ring and picked it as he was boarding the plane back to Los Angeles.

"Thanks, Al. That's going to be very helpful.

"Pat, after I tell you what I have learned with this piece of information, you will be able to say to everyone that you have seen and heard everything."

"Okay, boss, I'm waiting."

"The father of the child was Carl Grand."

It was about thirty seconds before Pat spoke.

"All right, boss. I am shocked and I would never had imagined. But I'm not sure how that helps us. So, they had a kid and he was a dealer. That doesn't mean anything."

"You're right, Pat, only if we can show that she received money from a known drug dealer and never declared it."

"We could have done that before by subpoenaing her bank records."

"Yes, but then she would have known it was us. Now, the subpoena can come from the US treasury who has uncovered Grand's bank account and transfers."

The trial for Beatrice Yanotti never took place as she pleaded no contest and accepted a sentence of two years' probation, monthly visits with a parole officer, five hundred hours of community service, and payback of all taxes with interest.

Zuma was not happy that there was no jail time. He knew that she would probably start something else that was illegal, and he would keep the file open. She would probably see lots of her friends when she was doing her community service. He hoped he might see her on his morning runs, along with others picking up the trash on the shores of Santa Monica bay. Her silence during and after the trial gave him security in knowing she never realized that he had been involved in helping the US treasury discover her failure to report income and pay taxes. Claudia was going to be safe.

CHAPTER 25

Carmella said she could be at the Shangri-La restaurant in half an hour, so they decided to wait before they ordered. When she arrived, she looked excited and happy.

"Hi, everybody. How do you do. I just heard this version of 'What a Wonderful World' by Israel Kamakawiwo'ole. He's from Hawaii and the words at the end of the song are how I greeted all of you."

Zuma spoke. "Carmela, Louis Armstrong made that song famous before your Hawaiian singer recorded his version."

"I didn't know that, Joe. The thing about this version is that he says when people are shaking hands and saying, 'how do you do' they really mean 'I love you.' So again, I say to you all my friends, 'how do you do.'"

"Carmela, I will no longer feel like the guy in that song 'The Girl from Ipanema' who gets passed by."

"I don't get that reference. What does he mean?"

"In that song, there is this beautiful girl who walks by the guy and never looks at him."

"Pat, I guess you must feel that Carmela is finally looking."

"I think she is."

"I am definitely looking."

With Carmela's announcement they all clapped their hands, laughing, and began hitting the table.

"Boss, with four bodies, with different religions, with different genders and races, drug dealing, and false confessions this must be just like that movie you told me about. Is it…"

"No, Pat, this ain't Chinatown. We solve some of our crimes."

"I think the four of us should go into a night club and do our favorite songs."

"Great idea, Claudia. And we can invite Shankman, Edwards, and Avril Kouri and they all will be saying 'how do you do.' The new baby in town can't talk yet and greet us but we now know is Morris Shankman Kouri."

As Zuma was finishing up his early morning run, he saw the hobo lady. They stared at each other. It was like a moment before checkmate in chess. Zuma knew she would not go to the police with any videos of his handing out money to the homeless because that would also draw attention to her in any trial. The hobo knew that Zuma would not be bothering her because of his concerns with bad publicity about his treatment of the homeless. Zuma walked away knowing that it was just a matter of time before the woman would once again be involved in crime. He started thinking about how he was going to prepare.

It was Sunday and Zuma had the day off. He did not have his uniform on he and Claudia, after walking on the beach, were grabbing coffee and scones at a stand on the 3rd Street mall. Claudia wanted to see some new art book that she had heard about, so they walked into the Barnes and Noble bookstore.

Zuma noticed a man sitting at a table signing books. "Hi, how do you get your ideas for the mysteries you write?"

"I see things in the paper or on TV. I can get them from anywhere. Sometimes, I get them from movies. I'm never sure what is going to capture my imagination."

"I envy your ability to be imaginative. Do you like writing?"

"Yes, I do. And what kind of work do you do?"

"I work for the city. I wish you good luck with your book. I'm not exactly into reading mysteries."

As Zuma walked away, he wondered if the author knew how tedious, difficult, and challenging it was to solve crimes. He wondered if the author knew that truth was sometimes stranger than fiction and always more complicated than the imagination of the author. He envied the writer at the table who would always solve the crime he had created!

THE END